W9-CKH-609

THE
SILVER COW

A WELSH TALE

RETOLD BY SUSAN COOPER

ILLUSTRATED BY WARWICK HUTTON

Aladdin Paperbacks

for Zoë
from
S. C.

First Aladdin Paperbacks edition 1991
Text copyright © 1983 by Susan Cooper
Illustrations copyright © 1983 by Warwick Hutton

Aladdin Paperbacks
An imprint of Simon & Schuster
Children's Publishing Division
1230 Avenue of the Americas
New York, NY 10020

Library of Congress Cataloging-in-Publication Data
Cooper, Susan.
The silver cow: a Welsh tale / retold by Susan Cooper;
illustrated by Warwick Hutton. — 1st Aladdin Books ed.
        p.   cm.
Originally published: New York: Atheneum, 1983.
Summary: The father of a young Welsh boy gifted with a magic cow
manages to destroy all the good things the cow has brought to their lives.
ISBN 0-689-71512-9
[1. Folklore—Wales.]   I. Hutton, Warwick, ill.   II. Title.
[PZ8.1.C7863Si   1991]
398.2—dc20   [E]   91-234 CIP   AC

Once upon a time, high in the green hills of Wales, there lived a farmer named Gwilym Hughes. His small stone farmhouse was bleak and lonely, and his black cattle wandered the mountain.

Not far from his farm was a lake, up on a ledge of the mountain where you would not expect a lake to be. Today it is called Llyn Barfog—in English, "the bearded lake"—because of the starry white water-lilies that fringe its dark water. But the water-lilies were not there then.

Gwilym Hughes was a man with a heart as small and mean as his beady black eyes. Every day of the year he sent his small son Huw out to look after the cattle. Huw would rather have gone to school, like the boys in the village below the mountain, but Gwilym Hughes would have none of that. "I am a poor man," he said. "My son must work."

He would not even let Huw take his harp to the pasture, to make music while he watched the cows. "Do you want the cows dancing off the mountain?" he said. "I'm a poor man. It is milk for the market we need, not music in the empty air."

But every now and again, when his father was not looking, Huw would take his harp with him under his arm. Bronwen his mother noticed, but she said nothing. She only shook her head and smiled sadly, and gave him a hug.

Up on the mountain alone, Huw played his harp beside the lake, while the black Welsh cattle chewed away at the grass and paid him no attention. But suddenly one day he knew that somebody was listening, and he looked up from his music and saw a strange shining cow, looking at him from deep brown eyes.

Silver as a new coin the cow was, from head to tail, glinting in the sun. She bent her head when Huw's music stopped, and began ripping like the others at the tough mountain grass; but she never left his side, and followed him when he took the cows home.

She came to Huw too when he was milking the cows with his father, and she gave three times as much milk as any other of the cows, and it was three times as rich as theirs. Gwilym Hughes was delighted and astonished.

"Where did you get her, boy?" he said.

All at once Huw knew where the silver cow had come from.

"Out of the lake," he said. "She was sent by the magic people, the Tylwyth Teg."

"Rubbish!" said his father; but his small black eyes were glittering. "Don't you let her go, now. She is worth her weight in gold. If only I had more cows like her, I could—I could—"

"Could you send me to school?" Huw said.

His father laughed scornfully. "I could be a rich man!" he said.

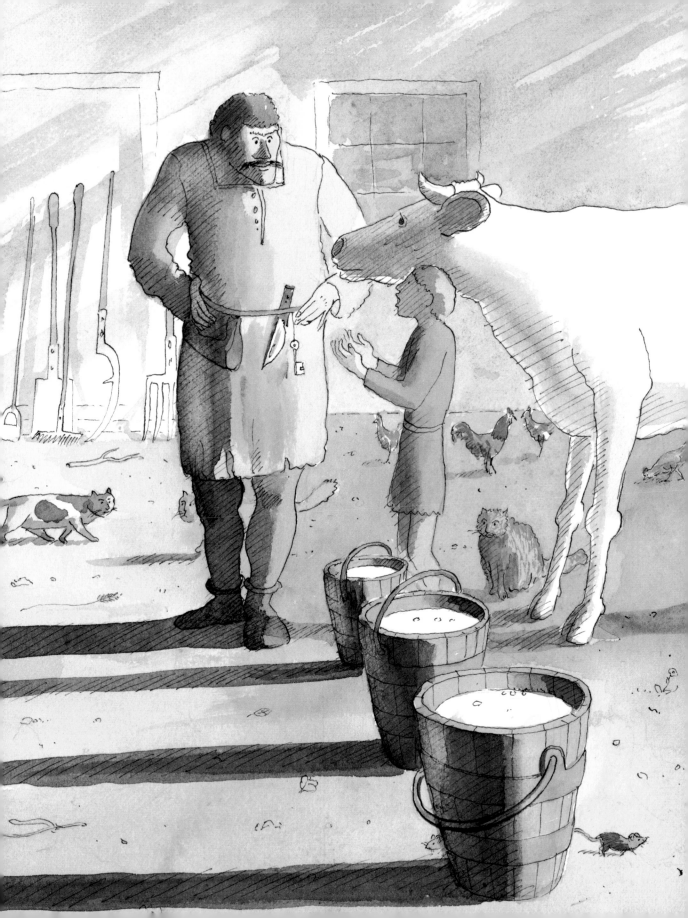

So Huw took the cows to the pasture every day, as always, and always the silver cow followed close, looking at him from her deep brown eyes. As the years turned, she mated with the black Welsh cattle, and every calf to which she gave birth was silver-gleaming as herself, and grew up to give milk as marvellous as her own.

Gwilym Hughes could hardly believe his luck. He became famous in the mountains for his milk and butter and cream, and soon he was very rich indeed. But still he would not release Huw from work, though he could have afforded ten cattle-men now. He bought himself a dark suit and a Sunday hat, and locked up his money in a great oak chest.

Often he went to the town, to brag of his silver herd to the other farmers, but he brought nothing back for Bronwen his wife but the coarse cloth from which she had always made her own clothes.

"This is for you," he said grandly just once when he came home, and he handed her a heavy iron thimble. Bronwen Hughes burst into tears, and her husband stalked angrily out of the room. But Huw, who was as big as his mother now, came to her and smiled sadly, and gave her a hug.

The silver cow seemed to grow no older, as the years passed, but she grew fat and slow, and gave no milk any more. One day Gwilym Hughes said, "It is time to take that one to the market. She gives no milk, why should we care for her now? To market with her — I shall be famous for my beef as well."

"Da," Huw said in horror, "you are not going to have her butchered?"

"Well, of course," said Gwilym Hughes. "What did you think I meant?"

"But you have no right," said Huw. "She is not yours. She is a magic cow, sent to us out of the lake by the Tylwyth Teg."

"Oh certainly," said his father with great scorn. "I suppose you have seen the Tylwyth Teg, and they told you that?"

"I have seen the waters of the lake quiver, when they were listening as I played my harp," Huw said.

His father glared at him in outrage. "Deceitful boy!" he shouted. "How dare you waste time on music when you should be watching my cows!" And he locked up Huw's harp in the chest with the money, and would not give it back.

A week from that day, the town butcher came up to the farm, with a group of inquisitive farmers following. Gwilym Hughes brought them out to the lake where Huw was watching the cows.

Huw saw them coming, and the light glinting on the butcher's big knife. In terror he flung his arms round the neck of the first silver cow. "Run away!" he cried. "Run!"

But the cow only looked at him out of her deep, dark eyes, and did not move.

"Oh Tylwyth Teg!" cried Huw to the waters of the lake, and to the clouds scudding low over the sky. "Help me! Tylwyth Teg!" But he had no harp to play the music that brought the Tylwyth Teg close, and they did not hear.

Then the farmers were upon them, with the butcher and his long knife. They clustered in a circle round the first silver cow, while she stood patiently watching them, making not a sound. Gwilym Hughes took her roughly by the horns, and the butcher raised his knife high, to cut her throat. Huw shouted in anguish, and leapt to seize his arm.

But suddenly then from the lake there came a voice: a high, unearthly voice. It was sweet as the song of a lark rising, but cold with rage.

"Come home, silver cows!" the voice called. "Come home!"

And as the long music of the calling echoed round the hills, the first silver cow broke away from Gwilym Hughes, scattering the circle of farmers, and she leapt towards the lake. After her, from all parts of the mountain, came all the silver cows that had been born to her, the treasures of Gwilym Hughes' herd. And one after the other, every one of them plunged into the dark waters of the lake, and disappeared. They were never seen again.

The lake lay quiet and secret, rippled by the wind.

"So much for Gwilym Hughes' fine beef," said one farmer to another.

"So much for his precious milk and butter," said a second. "They'll be no more now."

"Fooling with the Tylwyth Teg, isn't it?" said a third. "He's as greedy as he's mean."

As they began to straggle down from the mountain, Huw ran home. On the kitchen floor was the heavy oak chest, empty, with his harp lying free beside it.

His mother looked at him, dazed. "An echo of a voice there was, ten minutes past," she said. "And the lid of the chest flew off, and the money flew away."

Huw took his harp, and bundled up his clothes and some Welshcakes from the larder.

"I am flying away too, Mam," he said. "I am leaving him. Come with me."

His mother shook her head. "He will be a poor man again now," she said. "He will need me."

"He will never make you happy," said Huw.

"He is what he is," said she. "And I am too old now to leave. It is youth that should be free, like the music in the air. Perhaps that is what the Tylwyth Teg were telling him."

She gave Huw a hug. "God bless you, boy bach," she said.

Huw kissed her. "I shall live by my music, and learn," he said. "And come back for you some day."

Then he strode away from the farm, along the mountain road that runs past the lake Llyn Barfog. As he passed, he looked down at the water of the lake, rippling in the wind— and he stopped, surprised. All the dark surface was starred now with the broad floating blossoms of white water-lilies: one starry blossom for every cow that had vanished into the lake. Between the green hill and the grey sky they twinkled at him, in a bright farewell.

Huw stood looking, for a long time.

Then he went on and away, out into the world, playing
his harp in a farewell of his own to the silver cow of the
Tylwyth Teg.

THE END